Dino FC

THE UNLUCKY STRIKER

KEITH BRUMPTON

USBORNE

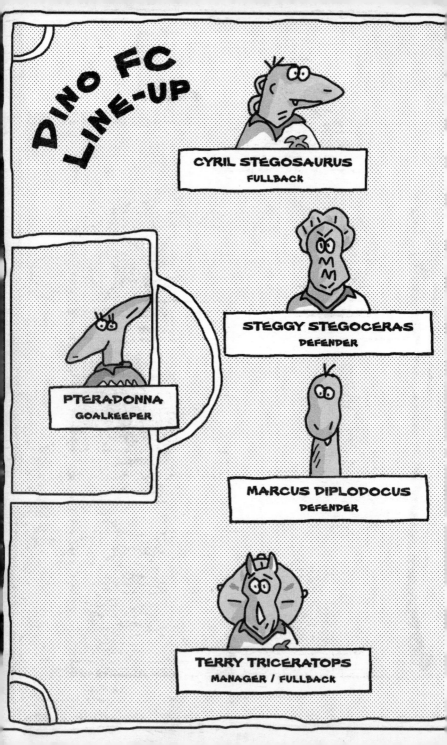

ARCHIE OPTERYX
LEFT WINGER

ALBERT ALLOSAURUS
CENTRE MIDFIELD

CELIA COELOPHYSIS
FORWARD

GWEN CORYTHOSAURUS
CENTRE MIDFIELD

JOSÉ HETERODONTOSAURUS
FORWARD

ERIC ALLOSAURUS
RIGHT MIDFIELD

TODAY'S SUB:

OLLIE OVIRAPTOR
FORWARD

Dedicated to Room 15, Mountview School,
Taupo, New Zealand

Go to www.keithbrumpton.co.uk
for more on Terry and the team.

First published in 2011 by Usborne Publishing Ltd., Usborne House,
83-85 Saffron Hill, London EC1N 8RT, England.
www.usborne.com

A CIP catalogue record for this book is available from the British Library.

ISBN 9781409538219

Dino FC were playing an away match at Volcano Valley, a big club with a stadium that was even closer to an active volcano than their own. The players could hardly see the ball for thick billowing smoke.

But despite the smoke and the heat, Dino FC were in fine form – especially their tricky young winger, Archie Opteryx.

Up in the commentary box, DBC (Dinosaur Broadcasting Corporation) experts, Gary Seymouria and Mark Megalosaurus, were enjoying Archie's display too (what they could see of it through the volcano smoke).

7

Every season the Dinosaur Players'
Association held a vote among its members
– the players – to decide who had been the
best footballer that season. And this year
Archie was everyone's lava-hot favourite.

Ninety minutes was up and the referee
was looking at his watch when Archie saw
the Volcano Valley goalie off his line
(munching some grass) and tried a long
range shot.

UH-OH!

The ball flew straight into the net. The ref blew his whistle. Five-one to Dino FC and a thirteenth goal of the season for Archie.

The team hurried to congratulate him for yet another match-winning performance.

But Archie was a modest young dinosaur and insisted it had been a team effort.

Hard-headed and grumpy defender Steggy Stegoceras agreed.

When they were back in the dressing room, player-manager Terry Triceratops thanked the team for their efforts.

"One of my tackles," chuckled midfield enforcer, Eric Allosaurus.

"Aaaarrh!" Slow-moving centre half Marcus Diplodocus suddenly gave a loud

cry from the showers. But it was only
because he'd turned on the cold water
instead of the hot.

Terry gave Archie a special pat on the
back.

(Terry expected hard work as well as skill from his team.)

Archie smiled.

"And I think the press want to talk to you," Terry said.

Archie suddenly looked worried.

Terry laughed. "It's nothing, honestly. You'll enjoy it."

But Archie didn't seem convinced. He headed to the press cave wishing he was relaxing back in the Volcano Valley clubhouse with the rest of the team.

A friendly pterodactyl led Archie to the large
press area where a bunch of sports reporters
had gathered to interview him.

"How does it feel to be favourite for the
DPA Player of the Year?"

"Er, great. But I haven't won it yet."

"Do you think one day you'd like to
move to a bigger team?"

Archie suddenly turned a paler shade of green. He hadn't realized that the goal was his thirteenth of the season. And he was a very superstitious dinosaur.

Long after the press conference had ended Archie was still thinking about how he had scored thirteen goals and how this might be unlucky.

What if he got injured, or lost form, or didn't score any more goals? This was a disaster of brontosaurus-size proportions! What was he going to do?

Archie didn't sleep all night for thinking about it, and was still worrying as the moon vanished and a pink and gold dawn stole over the horizon...

The rest of the Dino FC squad were
already training under Terry's watchful eye
as Archie hurried into view.

Archie was late and looked like he
hadn't slept all night.

Terry told him to join Gwen's team for a six-a-side.

GREAT, WE'RE BOUND TO WIN NOW WE'VE GOT ARCHIE!

But as Archie took the pitch, the thought that he had scored thirteen goals was still uppermost in his mind.

Marcus Diplodocus thumped the ball out of defence and it landed at Archie's clawed feet. Archie jinked past Albert Allosaurus's clumsy tackle and fired in a shot.

It hit the post and bounced away.

BAD LUCK!

Yes…bad luck, thought Archie. *It's just like that journalist said.* And for the rest of the training session, nothing seemed to go right for Archie. He hit the post again, and messed up a couple of dribbles, and then tripped over a tuft of grass when clean through on goal.

"Not your day today," said Cyril Stegosaurus.

And the more he fretted over his bout of bad luck, the worse Archie played.

It didn't escape Terry's notice. As soon as the training session was over he grabbed a quiet word with his underperforming forward.

NOT YOURSELF THIS MORNING, ARCHIE! NO INJURY WORRIES?

Archie shook his head and didn't offer any excuses. He was too embarrassed to mention that he was superstitious about his thirteen-goal tally. "Sorry, boss, I'll try harder next time."

Terry watched as Archie hurried off to the dressing cave. He worried that Archie didn't seem his usual chirpy self and mentioned his concern to Cyril Stegosaurus, his loyal number two and fellow fullback.

MAYBE HE WAS A BIT TIRED, BOSS? WE'VE PLAYED A LOT OF MATCHES LATELY AND HE'S ONLY GOT LITTLE LEGS.

Terry nodded. Perhaps Cyril was right. Not even top players can be at their peak every day.

HE'S A GOOD YOUNG PRO, WHY ELSE WOULD HE BE THE FAVOURITE FOR DPA PLAYER OF THE SEASON?

"It's not too late to vote for me," interrupted Steggy as he walked past.

Terry laughed. A little healthy rivalry was good for the team. But he hoped Archie would soon be back to his best – he was too important a player to lose form…

It was match day at Dino FC. Skinflint club chairman, Danny Deinonychus, was in his private tree box, talking on his shell-phone as usual.

IT'S A DISASTER – REPLICA SHIRT SALES ARE 3.2% DOWN THIS WEEK!

The prematch entertainment was just ending. The newly-formed Dino FC Cheerleaders were a bit clumsy but very keen and the fans applauded them even when they spelled the team's name wrong.

And now the stage was set for the match against Velociraptor Bay. Three points would take the team into the top six in the Dinosaur Premier League and Terry hoped Archie would be back on top form again.

But he wasn't on form at all... Archie spent the first half avoiding the ball. He never put his wing up for a pass. And every time there was a 50/50 ball he leaped out of the way.

The crowd normally loved watching Archie, but even they sensed something was wrong.

At half-time, high in their commentary box, top analysts Mark and Gary from the DBC had also noticed Archie's disappointing performance.

"We've not seen much of young Archie Opteryx."

30

Terry was asking himself the same question. For whatever reason, his brilliant young winger was out of the game and out of form. With the team trailing one-nil, and Archie still playing badly, Terry made the decision to take him off.

OLLIE! ON YOU COME!

Surprised look

JUST WHEN I'D PUT MY TRACKSUIT BOTTOMS BACK ON!

The fans were stunned to see one of their favourite stars substituted.

Ollie shook Archie's claw and ran onto the pitch.

Archie sat down on the bench. *I'm still stuck on thirteen goals,* he thought to himself, gloomily. *Unlucky thirteen. That's why I got substituted.*

WHAT HAPPENS IF I DON'T SCORE AGAIN? I COULD BE STUCK ON THIRTEEN GOALS FOR EVER!

After the substitution, Dino FC played much better. Ollie added his know-how to the forward line, even if his dodgy old knees meant he didn't have Archie's pace. Or even any pace at all.

But Velociraptor Bay had a well-drilled defence and held on for their one-nil win.

"If Archie keeps playing like a pair of Marcus's old pants then I'm still in with a chance of being DPA Player of the Season," announced Steggy to no one in particular.

Terry turned and applauded the home fans, who had never stopped chanting for the team, and then turned to Cyril, who was shaking his head ruefully.

"Something's not right," agreed Terry, "and I need to find out what it is...or I'm a striker down for the rest of the season..."

As the team drifted away from the ground,
Gwen and Pteradonna appeared next to
Archie and tried to cheer him up. They could
see he was still feeling down about the match.

"You speak for yourself," said Steggy Stegoceras, as he passed by.

Archie nodded. He was just about to tell them about the thirteen goals and how it was bringing him nothing but bad luck, when Marcus Diplodocus appeared saying he was very hungry and did anyone fancy going for a quick snack?

Archie made his excuses and left. On the way home a branch fell off a tree and landed on his foot.

More bad luck, he thought to himself.

He continued his walk home and tried to think of ways to protect himself against the bad luck he felt sure was coming his way...

CHAPTER 6

The day dawned warm and sunny. It was a perfect day for training, and normally Archie would have been looking forward to it all the way to the ground. But today he didn't have much spring in his step.

I hope I don't look too daft, Archie thought to himself as he stepped awkwardly onto the training pitch.

HOPEFULLY NO ONE WILL NOTICE ANYTHING DIFFERENT.

But there was no chance of that. Archie was greeted by grins and laughter.

The squad had immediately spotted that Archie was wearing the biggest pair of shin pads any of them had ever seen. They reached almost up to his waist.

"Expecting some bad tackles?" joked Gwen.

"He's lost it," sniffed Steggy with an unsympathetic tone.

Terry was puzzled too. His star player was certainly behaving very oddly just lately. He would have to have a quiet word later...

As for Archie's shin pads, well they certainly made him feel safe from being tackled. But the problem was he couldn't run in them. The pads were so huge they weighed him down, and then once or twice he tripped over altogether.

With the laughter of his teammates ringing in his ears, poor Archie felt he had no choice but to throw away the shin pads.

Except that then, of course, he was back to being worried about getting injured or being the victim of more bad luck. Every time the

ball came to him he passed it. Every tackle that came in, he jumped out of the way. And all the while his bad luck seemed to continue. He got an awkward bounce…

…Terry gave a goal kick when it should have been a corner…

...And he hit the post with a header.

My luck is getting worse, thought Archie and the more he thought about it the more it seemed to be so.

Terry watched his forward with concern. Archie's play wasn't getting better, it was getting worse!

After training Terry asked Archie into his
office cave.

"Take a seat."

"Thanks, boss."

Archie still felt nervous about admitting
unlucky thirteen was bothering him so much,
but he knew he could trust Terry to help. He
told him the whole story.

After Archie had explained, Terry sat

back in his chair and rubbed his chin thoughtfully. "I've heard of superstitious players before… I once knew a goalie who wouldn't walk under a crossbar, and at Iguanodon Thistle there was a player who always insisted on being last out onto the pitch."

BUT NEVER ANYTHING AS SERIOUS AS THIS.

Archie hoped his boss would be able to think of an answer.

Terry did. But it took him all day. And almost twenty-four hours had passed before Archie and Terry found themselves seated side by side in a neatly painted waiting cave just outside town. Archie felt nervous and fidgety, like he had a millipede in his pants.

"Neither am I," answered Terry, with his usual honesty.

Archie nodded and a few moments later a dilophosaurus wearing a black polo-neck jumper and gold medallion came across to them. He shook Terry's hoof.

He turned to Archie. "Then you must be he?"

Archie nodded.

Archie got up and followed.

"Good luck!" shouted Terry, sounding more confident than he felt.

Archie looked around the consultancy cave, which was painted a very soothing shade of blue.

"You're the hypnotist?" stammered a nervous Archie.

"Hypnotherapist," answered Darren, calmly.

I UNDERSTAND YOU HAVE A PROBLEM WITH THE NUMBER THIRTEEN. YOU CONSIDER IT UNLUCKY?

Archie nodded, feeling rather foolish. "Er, yes."

"Okay, well let's see what we can do to change that."

Archie felt suddenly hopeful.

"I want you to count to three, please, Archie. You *can* count to three?"

Archie nodded confidently. For a dinosaur he was very good at maths.

Archie was puzzled. He wasn't really feeling very sleepy yet.

"Try to relax."

Archie tried to relax. And this time he was more successful. In fact he fell off the couch and onto the floor.

MAN, THAT'S WHAT I CALL RELAXED!

Darren had to start the whole process again. But finally he had Archie hypnotized. Archie's eyes stared into space.

THE NUMBER THIRTEEN IS NOT UNLUCKY. YOU, ARCHIE OPTERYX, ARE NOT UNLUCKY...

Darren had hypnotized Archie to forget about bad luck but when he snapped his fingers to bring Archie out of the trance, would he have been successful?

Archie's chances of finishing the season on a high note were hanging in the balance...

Dino FC were training again. There were only two days left until their final match of the season and the announcement of the DPA Player of the Season.

The squad cheered good-naturedly when they saw Archie run onto the pitch without his giant shin pads.

CHEER!!

Terry stood on the touch-line, looking very nervous. If the hypnosis hadn't worked then he didn't know what he could do.

The squad divided into two teams for a practice match and it wasn't long before Archie got the ball. He sprinted confidently down the wing, and then executed a lovely body swerve as Eric Allosaurus stuck out a muscled leg to tackle him.

"So far, so good," smiled Terry.

"Thirteen minutes gone and he's playing well," added Cyril.

TH-THIRTEEN?!

Archie stopped in his tracks and a surprised Eric bumped into him.

WHUMPH!

Terry shook his head sadly as they pulled Archie to his feet. For the next few minutes a frightened looking Archie hardly touched the ball, preferring to stay out on the wing, avoiding any possible tackles.

While the players took a break to rehydrate (and José Heterodontosaurus called his agent) Terry waved Cyril over.

He told Cyril the whole story about Archie
convincing himself he would be unlucky as
long as he was stuck on thirteen goals.

"Looks like the hypnotherapy didn't work.
Unless we can solve this, I've lost my best
forward."

AND IT COULD
BE THE END OF
ARCHIE'S CAREER!

Cyril nodded. And then they both tried desperately to think of another plan. Cyril wasn't very good at thinking up plans as he had a smallish brain better suited to tackling opponents or eating bushes. But suddenly another scheme came to Terry.

CYRIL, HAND ME THAT TRAINING BIB, PLEASE...

AND THEN YOU KEEP THE TEAM OCCUPIED FOR TEN MINUTES OR SO. I'LL BE RIGHT BACK!

Before Cyril could ask any questions
Terry had run off, clutching the training bib.

OKAY, EVERYBODY, LET'S HAVE YOU DOING SOME SPRINTS TILL THE BOSS GETS BACK.

WHERE'S THE GAFFA GONE?

"I haven't a clue," answered Cyril,
truthfully...

CHAPTER 10

After practising their sprinting, Cyril got the squad practising "head" tennis, which was never easy because Marcus's head was so much higher than anyone else's.

He'd just accidentally headed the ball into the swamp when Terry finally reappeared. He looked hot and bothered and Cyril was surprised to see him wearing his tracksuit top.

Archie stared down at the ground. He'd been hoping he wouldn't have to play any more that day. Cyril watched his boss closely. He knew he must have something planned, he just couldn't work out what.

"Sure you don't want to take off your tracksuit top, boss?" asked Gwen.

Terry blew his whistle to start the game. And right from the off he dribbled the ball past five players and scored with a screaming shot.

Cyril said later he had never seen his boss play like this before. In fact none of the squad had. Terry was simply brilliant. He ran, chased, harried, dribbled, shot, tackled...

After just twenty minutes of play his team led ten-nil and Terry had scored six of the goals himself.

After scoring the latest of his goals, Terry turned and smiled at a dumbfounded Archie.

Archie nodded.

"Though I guess I was a bit lucky with that one that hit both posts before it went in?"

Archie shrugged.

"I'm glad you agree," smiled Terry. "Because I've always said you make your own luck in this game. I just wanted to prove it to you."

Archie looked puzzled.

Only now did Terry peel off his tracksuit top to reveal beneath it a training bib.

And on the training bib was printed the number thirteen.

"Number thirteen?" Archie looked puzzled. "But our squad numbers only go up to twelve."

EXACTLY. I HAD THIS BIB SPECIALLY PRINTED SO I COULD WEAR IT MYSELF AND PROVE TO YOU THAT THERE'S NOTHING UNLUCKY ABOUT THE NUMBER THIRTEEN!

Cyril, watching from across the field, grinned as he finally saw Terry's clever plan. Terry put his arm round Archie's shoulders.

Archie had no choice but to agree.

But deep down, Terry was wondering whether or not his clever trick really had given Archie his confidence back. Only tomorrow's big game would reveal the answer – and the stakes couldn't be higher!

Match day! The air was filled with the smell of hot fernburgers, the chanting of fans, swooping pterodactyls, and the excited chitter-chatter of the Dino FC squad as they arrived at Cetiosaur Celtic's impressive ground, ready for the final Dino Premiership encounter of the season.

Terry hadn't decided on his starting line-up yet. He wanted to try and gauge Archie's mood first. The early signs were good. The flying forward seemed more like his usual chirpy self as he helped Marcus look for his shirt. (It turned out Marcus was actually wearing it – back to front.)

Steggy was telling José he hoped Archie would play better than in recent matches.

But José wasn't listening, he was too busy asking his agent to try and get him a salary rise.

77

The ref blew his nose to begin the match and right from the off the game was fast and furious. Cetiosaur Celtic were a very physical side and Dino FC didn't seem able to keep hold of the ball for long.

Archie didn't get his first touch for about ten minutes.

Terry laid the ball off to Gwen Corythosaurus. Gwen passed the ball to Archie, but it wasn't a great pass...

...the ball was too far ahead of him and much nearer to a Celtic defender. But Archie didn't hold back.

With all his old confidence Archie hurled himself at the ball, nicking it from his opponent's claws, somehow staying on his feet...

...and then whipping in a magnificent cross that José Heterodontosaurus should have scored from, if he hadn't been worrying about a grass stain on his shorts.

But it soon became clear that Archie was going to win every 50/50 ball that was going. Superstitious numbers forgotten, he was in determined mood and back to his brilliant best!

The other Dino FC players soon realized that Archie was back on form. They made sure he saw plenty of the ball and he responded by setting up all three goals the team scored.

Cross from Archie

1-0

2-0

Pass from Archie

3-0

Cushioned header from Archie

Three-nil flashed on the scoreboard at
the end of the game, and the small but
happy band of travelling Dino FC fans were
chanting Archie's name.

THERE'S ONLY ONE
ARCHIE OP-TE-RYX!

But would Archie's fellow players agree
when the DPA Player of the Season votes
were counted later that same evening?
Especially after his late-season blip in form.

Players from every team in the league were there; lanterns hung in the trees; beautifully prepared food and drink was served; and then finally, at the end of the night, came the announcement of the main award…

THE DPA PLAYER OF THE SEASON AWARD. PLEASE WELCOME OUR COMPÈRE…

MISTER MARK MEGALOSAURUS!

Applause

Mark Megalosaurus was wearing a bow tie that had taken him five hours to fasten, and in his claws he was holding a silver envelope.

NOT LONG TO WAIT NOW, FOLKS...

On each team's table, hearts beat a little faster as players wondered whether they might be Player of the Season...

Pterodactyl Flappers FC table

Mark opened the envelope and took out a small card on which was written the winner's name. His expression didn't change as he read the name silently to himself and then moved closer to the microphone.

Thud, thud, went every heart in the room.

THE DPA PLAYER OF THE SEASON IS...

There was a long silence. No one dared breathe and the only sound was Marcus Diplodocus munching on some ferns.

MMM...SPICY, BUT STILL VERY NICE.

Chomp

THE MAIN CONTENDERS

Mark looked down at the envelope
again…enjoying prolonging the tension.

THE WINNER IS…
ARCHIE OPTERYX
OF DINO FC!

Cheering and wild applause filled the
night air as Archie vanished briefly under a
sea of Dino FC players, all wanting to shake
his wing or slap his back.

Only Steggy remained in his seat.
"Typical. Just typical!"

MAYBE NEXT YEAR THEY'LL PICK A DEFENDER FOR A CHANGE.

Archie struggled out from beneath his excited teammates and made his way to the stage. He shook Mark Megolosaurus's claw, took his award and knew he had to make a speech. He was feeling more nervous than if he'd been taking a sudden-death penalty in a World Cup final.

I...I...I'D LIKE TO THANK YOU ALL FOR THIS AWARD. IT'S A GREAT HONOUR...

Everyone applauded.

"But I couldn't have won without my teammates." Archie waved to the squad and they applauded back – even Steggy.

"But the biggest thanks of all has to go to someone who helped me through a really bad spell..."

SOMEONE WHO HAS ALWAYS HAD FAITH IN ME...

Archie pointed his shining new trophy towards Terry.

THANKS, BOSS... YOU'RE THE BEST!

And as camera flashlights popped and everyone applauded, Archie raised aloft the Player of the Season trophy and felt prouder than he'd ever felt in his whole life.

THE END

CHECK OUT MORE CRAZY FOOTY ACTION IN:

TERROR ON THE TRAINING GROUND

Dino FC's tough new trainer is trying to lick the team into shape. Can the players beat the flab and avoid the drop?

ISBN 9781409504832

THE MISSING FANS

Dino FC's fans have deserted them, but Terry's got great plans to attract new supporters... if only the players could remember his instructions!

ISBN 9781409504849

THE GREAT KIT CATASTROPHE

Dino FC's old kit is falling apart at the seams. But the new kit is a catastrophe. Are the team's chances of victory in tatters again?

ISBN 9781409504856

THE VANISHING GOALIE

Could rival team manager, Alex McTeeth, have anything to do with the mysterious disappearance of Dino FC's flying goalie?

ISBN 9781409504863

TRANSFER TROUBLE

The Dino FC players are stunned by Danny's shock announcement. What will they do without their star teammate?

ISBN 9781409538202

For more action-packed reads head to
WWW.FICTION.USBORNE.COM